For JG. Love you to Mars and back. —K.L.G.

To NASA's Mars Exploration Rover team.
Stay curious! —S.M.

The author would like to thank Dr. Tanya Harrison,
planetary scientist and director of research at ASU NewSpace,
for lending her expertise to this project.

THIS IS A BORZOI BOOK PUBLISHED BY ALFRED A. KNOPF

Text copyright © 2020 by Kristin L. Gray
Jacket art and interior illustrations copyright © 2020 by Scott Magoon
Interior photographs © NASA/JPL-Caltech/MSSS

All rights reserved. Published in the United States by Alfred A. Knopf, an imprint of
Random House Children's Books, a division of Penguin Random House LLC, New York.
Knopf, Borzoi Books, and the colophon are registered trademarks of Penguin Random House LLC.

Visit us on the Web! rhcbooks.com

Educators and librarians, for a variety of teaching tools, visit us at RHTeachersLibrarians.com

Library of Congress Cataloging-in-Publication Data is available upon request.
ISBN 978-0-525-64648-8 (trade) — ISBN 978-0-525-64649-5 (lib. bdg.) — ISBN 978-0-525-64650-1 (ebook)

The text of this book is set in OCR A Tribute and ITC Charter.
The illustrations were created using a Wacom Cintiq drawing tablet and an iMac running Adobe Photoshop.

MANUFACTURED IN CHINA
March 2020
10 9 8 7 6 5 4 3 2 1

First Edition

Random House Children's Books supports the First Amendment and celebrates the right to read

ROVER THROWS A PARTY

Inspired by NASA's *Curiosity* on Mars

by **Kristin L. Gray**

pictures by **Scott Magoon**

JULY 27

Rise and shine!
Time to capture another sunrise.

On Mars, sunrises and sunsets appear blue, while the daytime sky is rust. Fine dust particles in the Martian atmosphere absorb blue light and scatter warmer colors like red and orange. This makes

JULY 28
Another morning, another trek up
Mount Sharp. Wow! What a view.

Also known as Aeolis Mons, Mount Sharp is 3.4 miles
(5.5 km) high and rises from the center of the Gale Crater.
Traveling a short distance each day, the rover will take
years to reach the summit.

JULY 29

Took a selfie with a dust devil.
He really dug my invitation.

Twisters form on Mars the same as they do on Earth—when a rising, rotating vortex of hot air sucks up dust and dirt from the ground.

JULY 30

Maneuvered across rocky
terrain to collect soil samples.
Found a pet rock, too.
Wanted: a tiny party hat.

The rover scoops and shakes a small amount of soil into its belly, which is equipped with a mini-oven. Once heated, the dust breaks down, giving off fumes. These fumes are analyzed for hints of organic (living) compounds.

JULY 31
Zapping meteorites with my
ChemCam laser and dreaming
of birthday candles.
Oops.

The Chemistry and Camera
Complex fires a laser at rocks to
examine the vaporized material.
It can identify the type of rock,
the mineral makeup, and whether
water molecules or hazardous trace
elements are present.

AUGUST 1
Dance break!
Radio transmission
to Earth a success!

It takes approximately twenty minutes for a radio transmission from Mars to reach Earth.

AUGUST 2

Say "cheese"! It's Picture Day. I'm trying out all seventeen of my cameras. Want them working for my big par-tay.

ChemCam

Right NavCams [2]

Right MastCam

Right and Left Front HazCams [2 pairs]

CLIK
CLIK
CLIK

MALHI

– Left NavCams [2]

– Left MastCam

Because the rover's arm isn't long enough to capture the entire robot in one shot, a series of images is stitched together to make a self-portrait.

MARDI

AUGUST 3
Regional dust storm.
Thank goodness my big
bash is still two days away.

Dust covers can be flipped closed
during regional dust events to protect
the rover's optics, or camera lenses.

AUGUST 4
Prepping my broom in case
anyone decides to drop by.
Say tomorrow. At two o'clock.
Got that, universe?

FFtFFtFFt

The rover's Dust Removal Tool sweeps layers of dust off Martian rocks, giving scientists on Earth a better look.

AUGUST 5
Happy Mars-iversary to me! I landed on
August 5, 2012. Hey, NASA, how about that
virtual cake?

A Martian sol lasts twenty-four hours, thirty-nine minutes, and thirty-five seconds. That makes the day forty minutes longer on Mars than on Earth.

Ack! Spooked by my own shadow. That happens when you're the ONLY ONE on a planet.

Shadows are made on Mars in the same way they are formed on Earth, by an object blocking the light. In this case, the rover is blocking sunlight.

YOU'RE INVITED

Nothing to see here, just me, all alone, sweeping . . . rover tracks!

Another. Rover. I repeat: ANOTHER ROVER. How do my antennae look?

The straight lines that appear in the rover's zigzag tracks are actually the Morse code characters (• – – – / • – – • / • – • •). These symbols stand for JPL, NASA's Jet Propulsion Laboratory, where the rover is managed. The rover measures these marks in the terrain to determine how far it has traveled. This is called visual odometry.

Rovers throw the best parties in the universe.

Time to power down.
Rover to Command Central:
Requesting buddy backup
for tomorrow's tasks.

The engineers who control the rovers work through the night to plan and code every second of the rovers' day in advance.

AUTHOR'S NOTE

Imagine trying to hit a hole in one with a golf ball from Los Angeles all the way to Scotland. Impossible, right? Well, that's the amount of precision NASA's engineers needed in 2012 to safely land their new car-sized rover on Mars. Named by sixth-grader Clara Ma of Kansas in a nationwide essay contest, the *Curiosity* rover became the first Mars Science Laboratory (MSL) on wheels.

In an audacious landing involving cables, a rocket-powered sky crane, and the largest parachute ever flown, *Curiosity* touched down on the Red Planet at 10:32 p.m. PDT on August 5, 2012. Engineers at NASA's Jet Propulsion Laboratory in Pasadena, California, whispered or paced back and forth like worried parents for seven harrowing minutes, awaiting confirmation of its landing. Meanwhile, space enthusiasts gathered at live watch parties across the globe, like the one in Times Square, or sat at home in the dark, glued to their screens.

Curiosity's self-portrait with Martian sand dunes. This scene combines fifty-seven different images.

Finally, after traveling 154 million miles between the two planets, a black-and-white thumbnail image appeared.

"It's a wheel!" cried an engineer.

Indeed, *Curiosity*'s wheels had safely reached the surface of Mars.

Curiosity's first picture on Mars

This first image was only the beginning. Budgeted at 2.5 billion dollars, with an estimated life of two years, the nuclear battery–powered *Curiosity* has already surpassed its projected run. It has collected thousands of images of Mars, has discovered evidence of ancient Martian lakes, and has found briny (salty) water below the planet's surface. It has traversed the Gale Crater and explored the rocky terrain of Mount Sharp.

Foothills of Mount Sharp

An iron meteorite discovered by *Curiosity*

Curiosity's tracks

By drilling into Martian rocks, it has found phosphorus, nitrogen, oxygen, and carbon—raw ingredients necessary for life. While the amount of radiation measured by *Curiosity* is not acceptable for humans, *Curiosity*'s findings can help scientists plan safe manned missions to Mars in the future.

Lest you think *Curiosity* is all work and no play, it has enjoyed one bit of fun thanks to its savvy and spirited engineering team. To celebrate *Curiosity*'s first year on Mars, technologists at the Goddard Space Flight Center in Greenbelt, Maryland, programmed it to hum "Happy Birthday" on August 5, 2013. This marked the first time a song was played on another planet and, on a lesser note, inspired me to tell this story. At the time of writing, NASA has one working rover (*Curiosity*), plus three retired ones (*Sojourner*, *Spirit*, and *Opportunity*), on Mars, with plans to launch a fifth rover in 2020. *Curiosity*'s mission is to find out if Mars is, or was, suitable for life, thereby preparing the way for humans to one day explore Mars.

BIBLIOGRAPHY

Bowater, Donna, and Amy Willis. "Nasa *Curiosity* Landing: As It Happened." *The Telegraph*. August 6, 2012. Web. telegraph.co.uk/news/science/space/9454930/Curiosity-Mars-Landing-as-it-happened.html

Koren, Marina. "Why the *Curiosity* Rover Stopped Singing 'Happy Birthday' to Itself." *The Atlantic*. August 10, 2017. Web. theatlantic.com/science/archive/2017/08/why-the-curiosity-rover-stopped-singing-happy-birthday-to-itself/536487/

mars.nasa.gov/msl

Miller, Ron. *Curiosity's Mission on Mars: Exploring the Red Planet*. Minneapolis: Twenty-First Century Books, 2014.

Owen, Ruth. *Exploring Distant Worlds as a Space Robot Engineer* (Get to Work with Science and Technology). New York: Ruby Tuesday Books, 2016.

Pearlman, Robert Z. "Mars Rover Tracks Spell Out Morse Code Message." *The Christian Science Monitor*. August 23, 2012. Web. csmonitor.com/Science/2012/0823/Mars-rover-tracks-spell-out-Morse-code-message

Rusch, Elizabeth. *The Mighty Mars Rovers: The Incredible Adventures of Spirit and Opportunity* (Scientists in the Field Series). Boston: HMH Books for Young Readers, 2012.

CURIOSITY ROVER FACTS

Length: 10 feet (3 m)
Width: 9 feet (2.7 m)
Height: 7 feet (2.1 m)
Weight: 2,000 pounds (907 kg)
Length of arm: 7 feet (2.1 m)
Top speed: 2 inches (5 cm) per second

CURIOSITY'S CAMERAS

MARDI (Mars Descent Imager)—photographed the rover's landing.

MAHLI (Mars Hand Lens Imager)—located at the end of the rover's arm; takes high-resolution images in color.

ChemCam (Chemistry and Camera Complex)—a remote microscopic imager used to document laser spots made by the rover.

HazCam (Hazardous Avoidance Camera, 8 in all, 4 in front + 4 in back)—takes pictures of the terrain; located near the rover's wheels to watch out for obstacles or drop-offs.

MastCam (Mast Camera, 2)—takes color images and video for geological study; pictures can also be stitched together for a panoramic view of the landscape.

NavCam (Navigation Camera, 4)—located on the mast; used to drive the rover.